Imvula, Child of the Rain

To Chiara,

I hope you love this book as
much as I do & it brings
a little bit of Africa all the
way to Scotland.

love Nina

X

Imvula, Child of the Rain

Mark Gillies

ATHENA PRESS
LONDON

ISBN 10-digit: 1 84401 965 9
ISBN 13-digit: 978 1 84401 965 6

First Published 2007 by
ATHENA PRESS
Queen's House, 2 Holly Road
Twickenham TW1 4EG
United Kingdom

Printed for Athena Press

A story for Natasha

My dear Natasha,

Many months have passed since I bid you farewell one cold winter's day and promised to see you again in a couple of weeks. I was wrong; instead of two weeks, nine months went by. But now I am back with dusty bags and stories of Africa. One of these stories is especially for you and tells of a little friend of mine.

A wise man once wrote that if someone should try to write a story for children, then they must write of what they have lived with and loved, not just what has been studied. If I am to tell you a truly good story, a story to fill your imagination and dominate your memory, then I must tell of what I love. Only then might I be able to help you see the inquisitive and slightly hairy trunk of an elephant; smell the warm, sweet scent of freshly dropped dung; and feel the movement of the hot gravel crunching under your feet.

I truly loved being in the Pongola Game Reserve, in a part of South Africa called KwaZulu-Natal. Should you travel there one day, as I hope you will, you will find majestic mountains, a bewitching lake, and bush (for that is what Africans call their countryside) teeming with animals and birds. I hold a great affection for the reserve and for the people who work there, but it was the elephants that were my constant companions. I spent so much time with them that they even filled my dreams, so that often I was not able to tell whether it was night or day, whether I slept or woke.

Elephants are very like us. They are children for many years because they have so much to learn if they are to become capable adults. They live in family groups and they each have very strong characters. Some are prone to anger, some interested by everything, others are shy, some could be called lazy. My favourite ones were very stubborn — like you when you want to get your own way!

If you won't tell anyone, I will tell you a secret. Elephant rangers are not supposed to have favourites, but I did and he was a naughty little male elephant called Imvula. The story that follows tells of Imvula one very special day.

I hope you enjoy this tale from a little piece of the African bush.

All my love.

Uncle Mark

Cheshunt, 2004

The Beginning

I mvula was still not sure how he had come to be in the place of surprises in which he found himself. If he really worked hard on his memory, an act that made him stand very still and sway slightly, then it was possible to recall a time when he was very warm and very safe. It was very dark there, but he was always comforted by a regular gurgling and rumbling, underlain by a slow, powerful pulse, which all in all made it really very hard to stay awake.

He had liked this warm and dark place because, if he was honest, his second favourite past time – after playing –was sleeping. But it was getting a little confined and what he later learnt to call his legs did want to be stretched. So, when a crack of light appeared in his otherwise dark world, the unseen forces that pushed him towards the unknown did not concern him too much. You must not be surprised by Imvula's lack of fear, for if one thing is clear to all those who have come to know this little chap, it is that he is a very brave elephant indeed.

However, even brave elephants close their eyes some-times, especially when they fall into a whole new world. Slowly, opening first one eye and then the other, Imvula wondered where all the darkness had gone. In its place a grey sky stretched far overhead and he blinked because the

light from this sky hurt his eyes. Of c...
know the sky was so called, nor did he kn...
that the waving green fronds that seemed...
were trees; he only knew this when he was...
we are looking back at his memories of Th...
so can use the wisdom of a slightly older el...

Imvula did not stare at the sky for long, what interested him the most were the large brown figures that stood, swaying in a close circle around him. Four massive legs supported a great body which in turn held an impressive head. Each head had two large ears, watchful eyes and an amazing trunk that seemed to be able to move in all directions.

The figure closest to him had lowered its head and was using its trunk to touch Imvula, stroking away the mess which covered his skin, while insistently prodding and pulling him to his feet. Eventually, Imvula stood, slightly unsure, but still very brave in the shadow of this figure. The trunk refused to leave Imvula but he was happy, for the smell was familiar and he was sure that this animal had something to do with the warm, dark place from which he had emerged. In fact, somehow, as he absorbed the rumbling of the gathered elephants, the creak and swish of the surrounding trees, and the evidence of the birth lying at his feet, Imvula suddenly understood that he was an elephant. Not only was he an elephant, but so were the figures who surrounded him. What is more, the mass under which he stood, where he knew he could always go if he did not feel brave, was his mother.

The elephant that sheltered our brave little hero, and encouraged him to feed on the rich and warm milk her body was storing, was known as Curve. She was very tired at this time, having carried Imvula within her for twenty-

.ths; but she was content, for her son was safe and now take his place in the little community of eleants, which she had heard the men in their green vehicles call 'The Orphans'. As she stood, gaining strength from the company of her sisters and cousins, water fell in steady drops from the grey sky. The drops gathered in the wrinkles of her skin and ran in rivulets down onto the small back of her son, further cleansing him and leaving him appearing like a shiny grey pebble in an expanse of turned earth.

Curve rumbled softly and informed her gathered family: 'It seems that the rain does indeed bring new life. Therefore I must name our new life after the rain that marks this special day.' This all took place in Zululand and so we must use the language of the Zulu. Therefore our little brave elephant became known as Imvula, meaning 'rain'.

Imvula was not sure whether he liked his name. As the days went by he thought he should have a name that reflected the fact that he was a very brave elephant indeed. He wanted to be called Warrior or Mammoth, but after a while he grew to like Imvula, for everyone was always very pleased when the rain came and he wanted people to be very pleased when he was around. So the name stuck.

Imvula was now free to explore this new world. Each day provided new surprises: seemingly solid logs would collapse under his weight; long grass concealed strange, flying creatures; or tree stumps that tried to trip him up. Sometimes the earth under his feet would fall away, revealing a network of mysterious tunnels. So great was his fascination for these endless discoveries that Imvula began to forget about the warm, dark place from which he came. Indeed, it was only when a cold wind blew from the mountains, carrying with it tales of snow and cold oceans, or when forks of lightning split the night sky, that Imvula

longed for the safety of the time before The Beginning. Even then, all he had to do was to seek out the comfort of his mother. Her loving touch and steady eyes brought reassurance that it was all right not to be very brave all the time.

This, then, is our introduction to Imvula, Child of the Rain, and a very brave elephant indeed. However, we must now jump forward in time. Hold on tight as we fly through time to a day when Imvula was nine months old and Christmas was soon approaching. As we fly, first fix in your mind's eye a picture of Imvula, for he is our hero and it is only right that you carry a picture of the hero. Then, should you meet him one day, you will be able to greet him appropriately.

Baby elephants can fit under their mother until they are about a year old. In appearance, they are very similar to the adults, though lacking the fearsome tusks that can grow to such remarkable proportions. However, if you look closely, you can see that some things are not quite right. The four legs are a little too long for the body and so their rear end and shoulders are sloped; because of this, the body always appears to be a little behind the ambition of the legs when the baby elephant starts to move.

It takes a long time to learn how to use the trunk; it is a little like when we humans struggle to learn how to write. Months must pass until the little elephant can achieve simple tasks – like lifting its trunk to sniff passing smells – and it will be nearly a year before they can use the trunk to pull leaves from branches, or grass from the ground.

Lastly, an elephant's eye never grows; it is the same size for the infant as for the adult. This means that baby elephants appear to have very large eyes. They appear to be innocent creatures, but rest assured, mischief is never far away!

All of this applies to Imvula. He is small and rounded with long legs that propel him over the ground at a speed slightly too fast for him to control. His trunk is alive and also very uncontrolled compared to those of his mother or aunts. He is grey but, as he is normally covered in dust and mud from his various adventures, he often appears in changing shades of brown. He has large, brown eyes and holds his head high, for he knows it is his job to be alert for danger. But, most importantly, he is very, very brave. Do not let anyone tell you otherwise.

Dawn

Night in the Pongola Game Reserve is not the same night you see when sleep proves a little hard to come by and you kneel upon your bed, prop your elbows on the window sill and stare out towards the lights of London. Night, to you, is only midnight blue at the very height of the heavens; elsewhere there is always an orange glow creeping up from the horizon, so it is never really dark at all.

In Pongola, and throughout the African bush, how much you can see during that period between the setting of the sun in the evening and its glorious rise in the morning is determined by the moon and by the clouds. The moon, like in our home skies, passes through a sequence of phases, before being renewed by the passage of a month. But in Africa the moon has no competition; it is the greatest source of light in the night sky. When the moon is full and appears to all the people below to be a large circle of cheese, night challenges day and it is even possible to read a book by moonlight and not need a torch. As the movement of our planets causes the moon to appear to shrink, the light fades until, when there is no moon, the night is truly black.

However, this beautiful world in which we live is kind to us, for though we lose the moonlight, nature provides a glorious twinkling replacement. When there is no moon, it is possible to see all of the stars; each one a small source of light, making the sky appear as a velvet coat studded with all the diamonds of the world. If you think back to when I showed you a map of South Africa, you will remember that it is across the other side of the world to our small island. South Africa is so far away that it even has a different sky, with many more stars than our northern skies. Many people believe that the stars tell stories of our history and may even contain the secret of our future. But I was just happy to enjoy their beauty and play with the patterns in the sky, linking the distant twinkles until they made one sparkling picture.

On some nights layers of cloud stretch across the night sky and then both the moon and the stars are hidden from the earth. On these nights there is no light from the heavens and no light escaping from the homes of men scattered through the bush. Complete darkness then settles across the land; it is as if all the light has been stolen from the world. It is towards the end of one of these nights that our journey through time slows and we join Imvula.

The place of trees was not where Imvula liked to spend these nights without light. There never seemed to be enough room for him. Wherever he wandered he came upon spiny obstructions as young acacia trees and spindly sickle bushes blocked his path. Then, of course, there was the problem of getting around one of his aunts when she decided to feed upon some choice bark or the leaves on the trees that had recently begun to shoot.

However, with his head down and led by his faithful trunk, he slowly picked his way along the narrow path that seemed to offer the easiest way through the thick bushes. Imvula had long ago decided that his trunk was not really a part of him in the same way that his legs were. This was because it would never do exactly what he wanted. In the beginning it just lay limp in front of him, occasionally rising to catch the wind, but nowhere near as useful as the trunks belonging to his aunts. They could smell, touch, break branches and strip leaves with their trunks, but, more importantly, they could make amazing, twisting shapes. So Imvula had instead decided that his trunk must be treated patiently, as a slightly stupid friend who tries hard but is not quite able to achieve his aim – a bit like his cousin, Pixle. This arrangement had worked admirably and now Imvula and his trunk were firm friends. In fact, lately, Imvula was inclined to think that his trunk was becoming more skilful and may one day be able to do exactly what he wanted.

The branches gave way before Imvula's progress and he found himself in what he thought must be a clearing. It was still so dark that it was difficult to see how far away the branches were that waited for him. That was another reason that Imvula disliked the woods; the branches did not smell like the other animals that shared his world and they made little noise. They only made a noise when they were being broken or scratched against some part of his body, and by then it was too late to avoid their persistent attention. You see, Imvula's eyesight, like that of all elephants, was not too good; he found it much easier to smell and to hear than to see.

Pausing to make sure the darkness held no nasty surprises, Imvula listened with satisfaction to the sound of breaking branches and caught the familiar scent that told him of the presence of his mother. As he drew closer to the noise her solid outline became clear against the early morning sky, which, though still very dark, held just a hint of the approach of dawn. With his trunk now lying obediently flat on his head, Imvula ducked under his mother's forelegs and probed around in the warm dark until he found the milk that his stomach had been telling him to look for all the past hour. Imvula was of the age where he had started to eat a small amount of leaves and tug tufts of long green grass out of the soil, but it was more in imitation of his surrounding family than serious eating. In his opinion, it was still impossible to beat warm, fresh milk, straight from his mother.

Imvula's mother, Curve, was still as relaxed as the day she had produced her firstborn. She had to be, for Curve was the matriarch of the small family group. This meant that she was the leader, responsible for the protection of the group, deciding where to spend the days and the source of all important knowledge, which elephants need if they are to stay healthy in hard times. Her name reflected her left tusk, which curved to rise above her right one. Though she was only a young elephant, the deep wrinkles running across the top of her trunk made her appear older than her seventeen years. Imvula thought her to be the most beautiful elephant in the world, and when her eyes have gazed deep into your eyes, unconcerned and completely calm, I think you will too.

'Mum,' said Imvula, licking away the last of the milky froth which threatened to escape his greedy tongue, 'where are we going to go today? I want to go swimming. My trunk is becoming full of dust and you know that I have trouble reaching the water in those round ponds that the humans built.'

'Well, my dear,' replied his mother, chewing steadily, 'this may be a very special day, so we must just see what happens. We shall eat well, move, and perhaps drink a little, as we usually do. There will not be time to go as far as the lake shore for a little swim, nor, before you ask me, will you be able to play with the bush buck in the Fever Tree Forest.'

Imvula was very disappointed and tried to disappear back

in the direction of the source of the milk, but Curve had shifted to reach a slightly higher branch and so he merely walked headfirst into her front leg. Reversing quickly, and trying to fix his mother with the power of his full stare, he replied, 'What is so special that I can't go swimming?'

'You'll just have to wait and see,' Curve murmured, her mouth filled with the results of her trunk's persistence. 'What may happen today is so special that you must see it for yourself without warning from me.'

The wisdom of this answer was lost on Imvula, who did so want to go swimming. Swimming meant a trip all the way down to the shoreline of the lake, which stretched further that his eyes could see. All of the elephants became excited when they went swimming; they forgot to be boring and responsible and played in the same manner as all the young elephants. Imvula had even seen some of the young bulls, males like him, pushing each other's head under the surface of the water and climbing on each other's backs. So, disappointed, but determined to find the nature of this 'special' something, Imvula left the clearing and went to find the others.

He moved slowly, still relying on his friend the trunk and his ears more than his eyes, as it remained very dark. Elephants do not sleep for a long time during the night as we humans do. Instead they take little naps throughout the day and continue to move and feed throughout the night. Just then, if Imvula had known this, I think he would have preferred to be a human sleeping soundly, for suddenly his front legs gave way and he fell into a hole.

'Oi!' said a sharp little voice. 'Get out of my hole!'

With back legs resolutely reversing and front legs scrabbling to get a purchase on the treacherous surface, which had sent him toppling into the hole in the first place, Imvula scrambled out of the hole and shook the mud from his face. He spun angrily, ears outstretched and head raised, towards the source of the voice. As he peered into the gloom, Imvula wished he had the strength and imposing presence of a big elephant.

What Imvula saw caused him to start in surprise. A small hunched figure was squatting on the ground. It had a long snout, long pointed ears and a thick tail, tapering to a point. It may once have had a lovely coat like some of the animals Imvula had seen before, but now could only boast a pale grey skin, decorated with sparse hairs.

'I said, that's my hole! I dug it and I want to dig some more. There are some fine ants in there and I am hungry, so beat it! All an aardvark wants is a bit of peace; but no, a blooming elephant has got to come bumbling around. I mean, when I was a boy…'

'So you're an aardvark!' Imvula exclaimed. His head dropped slightly as he was pretty sure there would not be any fighting to be done, but his ears remained spread, just to ensure this funny creature did not do anything stupid. 'I know about you. You're the one who digs all these holes in the road and who nobody ever sees.'

The aardvark stopped snuffling in the piles of topsoil and drew himself proudly up to his full height (which was still some way short of the recently toppled baby elephant!). 'That is me and proud to be. The finest diggers of holes this side of Cape Town. Any type of hole you want as long as it is a test pit, a feeding pit, or a nice little place to live. We do conversions, but not if there are any bleedin' snakes around.' He paused. 'You can't have that hole, I only just dug it.'

'I don't want it. What do I want with a hole? There are so

many that I'll fall in the next one if I want to. In fact when I am a big elephant, with tusks and everything, you'd better not still be digging holes. Because if you are I will come and find you and then you'll be sorry… But that is not the point, do you know why it is a special day today?' asked Imvula.

'Oh, I see,' said the now affronted aardvark, 'first he threatens me and then he wants my help. Do they not teach you young elephants any manners any more? I ought to have a word with your mother.'

'Please don't, Mr Aardvark,' rushed Imvula, who, despite being a very brave elephant, knew what his mother's response to proven bad manners would be and was anxious to avoid her disapproval. 'I just want to know what could be more special than me, for one day I will be a big bull elephant and those funny people will travel from far away to see me.'

The aardvark softened his tone and said, 'I'm sorry son, but you are going to have to ask someone else. You see I go to bed as soon as the light comes and so I only ever hear tales of what *has* happened, not what is going to happen. Make sure you tell me though. You promise?'

Imvula, disappointed once more, mumbled his agreement and wandered further along the path. Somebody must know what the special event would be and he was determined to find out.

By now the dark night was beginning to loosen its grip on the world. Its closed fist was open and the spread fingers retreated across the sky, pursued by the rising sun, herald of both heat and colour for the approaching day. If Imvula could have risen above the thicket of bushes and trees in which he was having such trouble, he would have seen the growing light revealing the bulk of the Lebombo Mountains, sides falling like melting ice cream after the scoop, to the narrow blue slash of the Jozini Dam. On one side of the dam, the slopes of the mountains were densely wooded. On the other, the home of the elephants, low hills rose and fell, obviously dry and lacking grass but still bearing thousands of trees and bordered by the vibrant green swathe of shoreline. Imvula was happier, for the growing light at least made it a little easier to navigate his way through the obstructive bushes. He had much to do if he was to find out why it was to be a very special day.

Family

I mvula had been born into a small family group of elephants that would live the length of their lives in extremely close contact. Only the male elephants must leave the family group, but not until they are about fifteen summers old. By then, if the truth be known, they are itching to get away and have their own adventures in new, unfamiliar lands. But for now, Imvula did not have far to go before he found a familiar brown rear end sticking out of a bush. The sound of movement and a host of familiar smells meant that he had found the rest of the group.

The rear end in front of him was supported by a back left leg, which had an old wound and was reluctant to take its share of the weight placed upon the other legs. This told Imvula all he wanted to know; he had found Constant, his favourite aunt and replacement mum, should it be just too much of an effort to seek the safety of his real mum. However, Imvula always felt a little silly talking to anybody's rear end and so he looked around for something with which to attract her attention.

Repeated scuffing of his front left leg in the dust of the path had prompted no reaction, but it did unearth a thin root, produced by one of the neighbouring acacia trees in an effort to gain more water from the soil. In co-operation with his trunk, Imvula gripped the root, lowered his head and, with all the power his nine months could muster, drew a great length of the root from the soil's embrace. Lifting it to head height, he then stumbled forward and, pulling the freed end of the root tight, ran straight into Constant. All that effort brought no response, so he reversed and tried again.

This time Constant stepped back from her breakfast, seemingly hidden somewhere within the heart of the bush, and looked lovingly, if slightly wearily, at her little nephew. She had, after all, heard him coming way back up the path and had listened with amusement to his conversation with the aardvark. Shifting her weight from one foot to another, her trunk reached out and affectionately ran over Imvula's head and finished by tickling under his forelegs.

'Yes, Trouble? What brings you and your root here?'

'I want to know what is happening today that is so special we cannot go to the lake and I cannot go swimming.'

'Ah, so your mother told you something special is to happen today. Well, I hope she is right.' Constant looked serious for a little while and her attention seemed to wander away from her inquisitive nephew. She was named after her regular and constant tusks. But she also wore a large collar which, according to the other elephants, the humans had placed on her, making her a very distinctive elephant. Her injury caused her pain, but she carried it without complaint and had, in fact, gained in size these past few months. 'But your mother would have told you everything if she wanted you to know, so I cannot say anymore. You will be a big bull one day, but a bull must be clever and strong if he is to become King of the Bush, so you must try to discover what could be so special.'

However vulnerable and appealing Imvula made himself appear, Constant refused to say any more on the matter.

Indeed, she rumbled to Curve to inform her where Imvula had got to. Curve and Constant had an extremely close relationship and would always be found near to each other in times of peace and in times of danger. Imvula glumly accepted that he would definitely not discover anything now and went to investigate the shadow of another approaching figure, in the hope of finding some answer there.

'Who goes there?' called a voice. A cloud of rising dust hid all but the ears of Pixle, Imvula's elder cousin by almost a year. 'You cannot pass without the password.'

'Black rhino.'

'That was yesterday's. There is a new one now.'

'I am not playing,' said Imvula. 'I am on a very important mission so let me pass.'

Pixle continued to block the road, pawing the surface, with his ears outstretched to their fullest extent. After all, he was the elder of the two and no young pipsqueak was going to tell him what was a game and what was not. He had, however, overlooked one important factor and that was that Imvula really was a very brave elephant indeed. He enjoyed fighting and he relished winning, especially against older elephants.

Faced with Pixle's obstruction, Imvula folded back his ears, gathered away his trunk, dropped his head and charged. In years to come such an action would spell great danger for any ill-positioned human, but for now it just sent Pixle stumbling off the path and onto an uncomfortable bed of prickly pears. Though Imvula was in a hurry on his important quest, he could not resist celebrating his victory by trying to mount Pixle, who was at that moment struggling to his feet. What a mistake! Pixle was just able to throw off the triumphant Imvula and send him toppling to

the ground. Unfortunately, the effort was so great that he also lost his footing and so he lay half on and half off the temporarily defeated Imvula.

There was a tense silence and the disturbed dust began to settle on the battleground. Just then, the leaves began to rustle and there could be heard the scrape of branches across hide. A small elephant slowly appeared, larger than the two young males, but still considerably smaller than Curve or Constant. The tips of two new tusks were just visible from the space below the trunk and it was possible to tell from the way she held her head that she was very proud of these tusks indeed. In fact, her whole manner was one of confident self-importance. The two boys groaned; it was their cousin, Charlie. She had been all right, for a girl, but since she had turned two years old – a fact nobody was allowed to forget – she had tried to act like an adult, and that had meant trying to control them.

Four well-manicured feet were placed gingerly upon the path and deliberately made their way towards the confused heap of elephants. The feet stopped and two eyes, unsure whether to pretend to be bored or to let their interest show, surveyed the two waiting elephants.

'And *what* are you two up to now?'

'Nothing,' was the shifty response.

'If you don't tell me now it will only get worse for you.' The two boys had to admit that one day Charlie was going to make a very good grown-up elephant, but they really wished it did not have to be this day.

Pixle was the first to crumble: 'Imvula started it. He attacked me; he is always attacking me.'

Imvula, while considering whether to make a fresh attack and so claim outright victory, decided against it and instead in a low voice confided the importance of his mission.

'Something *special* is going to happen today and I'm going to find out what it is.'

'Of course something special is going to happen today, it's a special day,' replied Charlie knowingly.

'They've told you?' demanded Imvula.

Charlie's face fell. 'Well, not exactly – and even if they had I could not tell – my mum just told me to be on my best behaviour and to make sure you two behaved as well. Something about, "having enough to worry about".'

Charlie's mum was called Charm. Though she was closely related to all the other cows (female elephants), she had an independent character and would often move quite far away from the group. She had been the first to have a calf (as baby elephants are called) and would sometimes tell her daughter a little more than the other cows thought appropriate. Charm had long tusks and was also very beautiful, with long eyelashes that at times almost completely covered her dark eyes.

Pixle wanted to talk about his mum, but Imvula was in a very strange mood and he did not like Charlie when she was being a know-all, so he just remained quiet. The truth be known, Pixle was not a very brave elephant. He preferred to explore the world that surrounded him rather than fight it, but he knew what was expected of a bull and so reluctantly found himself involved in brawls with his younger cousin. His mother was called Charisma. She had rips in her ears, lop-sided tusks with a groove running across the end of her right-hand one, but he loved her and he dreaded that far-off day when he would have to leave her care and travel alone.

By this time, Imvula had realised that his cousins were of no help to him and he very much doubted that any of the adults would be able to share the knowledge they all certainly held. Crinkling his forehead and concentrating very hard, he tried to think. To a brave elephant of action this was a very tiresome activity, which made him very hungry. He therefore stood up, informed his cousins that he did not want to follow that path anyway, and returned to his mother and the warm, satisfying milk.

He had wasted valuable time talking to his cousins and now was slightly concerned to find that his mother and the other females were much nearer the edge of the river line. They were, in fact, close to the place where there were less trees and bushes to be found and where there was more grass and space to grow. You see, one of Imvula's few fears was that he would not grow to be a big bull if he spent too much time in the confines of the bushes. However, his concern turned to anticipation – after, of course, he had drunk his fill and wiped his mouth – for he realised that it was in places like this that he often found those funny humans.

Imvula's luck had begun to change, for just then the wind began to blow from the direction of the open hillside. The wind is a friend to all the animals and they listen to her message very carefully. When she is kind, the wind brings warning of any new approaches. This is why animals do not mind greatly when the wind blows cold, for they remember the greater good it does them. On this day, the wind flew down his trunk and stroked his ears, allowing both smell and hearing to gleefully tell him of the approach of the humans in their familiar green vehicle.

Humans

The wind was not the only herald of the humans' approach, though it was normally the first – unless it was careless, or on other business, and blowing from another direction. The antelope would also warn the elephants, though Imvula was convinced this was mainly to show off. Kudu would bark, impala cough and wildebeest blow. For such pretty animals they made very strange noises; perhaps they were just trying to appear as fierce as his mother when she would shake the very leaves from the trees with the power of her trumpet. These concerns threatened to distract Imvula from the importance of his mission, but fortunately his trunk was paying attention and led him to the very edge of the treeline. Here Imvula peered along the road that wound its way up the hill and seemed to end in the sky itself.

Imvula was very careful to keep the rest of his body hidden by long, sharp-edged blades of grass, which seemed to package the base of the trees as they entered the dark brown earth. He knew the procedure: when humans appeared one of the adults must go to them first to see whether they were behaving appropriately and not threatening the family in any way. Should they present a threat, he would see the investigating elephant's tail rise, her back arch and her head raise. She would show the full extent of her ears and look really very fierce. Now, according to the rules, this meant Imvula should retreat and hide from the danger, but this was always a problem, for brave elephants do not hide.

However, on this day, Imvula obeyed the rules and remained hidden. He knew that his mother and aunts had also heard the approaching sound for their ears twitched, but otherwise they just continued to feed and move slowly through trees, which had thorns so swollen that they were known as belly thorns. The noise was growing constantly louder and sounded like the distant rumble of a far away elephant. Sometimes the noise faded and then returned a bit louder. Imvula did not fully understand the reasons for the changing level of the noise, but it always resulted in the arrival of the green truck and the people.

Today the rumble grew in volume slowly and Imvula could now just make out the shape of the approaching vehicle. The sun was climbing higher in the sky, its rays reflecting off the shiny bonnet, destroying any hope the humans may have had of making a secret approach. Some days the green vehicle would roar straight past the trees in whose cover the family stood, bucking and bumping as it encountered the aardvark's holes or ridges in the road, but today it was moving slowly and this meant it was looking for them. Humans were strange for many reasons; the most important being that they never appeared to eat. Still, they did move around a lot and so Imvula hoped that they might just be able to tell him why today was going to be such a special day.

The vehicle slowed to a stop close to where Imvula was hiding. Unlike most of the vehicles, which almost completely shielded their contents from the outside world, this one seemed to have nothing more than a large green front, four wheels and a long square rear. This was where the humans could often be seen, squatting like the monkeys when concentrating on a particularly tasty piece of fruit. There was always the same man in the front, but the number of people with him would change – all looking, sounding and smelling slightly different every time, and so normally worth investigating.

Imvula watched as his mother, Curve, abandoned the belly thorn that had held her attention for the past few minutes and moved in the direction of the sickle bush that grew towards the sky close to the halted vehicle. Imvula admired his mother's intelligence, for who would realise that she was actually going to investigate the green visitor? As Curve reached the bush she swung her head to face the people and stood directly opposite the man sitting at the front of the vehicle. There were no doors between this man and the elephants, so he was always a tempting target. However, much to Imvula's disappointment, the man had never tried to move and that was no fun. His mother towered above the vehicle, but said nothing.

There was no danger today. Although Curve remained close to the vehicle, she had turned away and really was feeding on the sickle bush now. Imvula took his opportunity, pushed the grass aside and moved into the open, careful to keep the bulk of his mother between him and the vehicle. To his right hand side he could see the top of Charisma's head and Charm could be heard rearranging the bushes off to his left. Constant remained in the cover of the river line – which was strange, as she was normally the first to investigate any new arrivals and often gently reprimanded Imvula for being too adventurous. Never mind, thought Imvula, maybe she finds the strong smell of the people tiresome and is just trying to avoid them today. Charlie and Pixle were out of sight, which disappointed Imvula. He wanted them to appreciate just how grown-up he could be. But he did not have time to waste: he must act, and quickly!

Nudging his head past the rear legs of his mother, Imvula avoided her swinging tail and watched the vehicle, careful to remain unseen. He could see the square end, the wheel and, if he stretched just slightly further, the back of the first person. This was no good; he would never be able to get a satisfactory answer from here. Just then Curve moved forward, already having lost interest in the humans, and targeted another bush (she really was hungry this morning).

Exposed, Imvula lost any further time to think as the humans all spotted him and, in their usual manner, opened their mouths and squawked excitedly. 'Aaawwwww.' The only thing more annoying to an elephant's ear than an excited human is a disturbed francolin. A francolin is a distinctive bird that rarely flies and spends a lot of time breaking open elephant droppings to see what lies inside, and eating anything of interest. To Imvula, humans and francolins managed to combine such curious and annoying habits that he was sure the two must be related in some way.

To counter the excitement of the humans, Imvula decided to let them know exactly who was boss. He planted his front feet wide apart, spread his ears and tossed his head. This did not have the desired effect. Instead, the squawking increased: 'Aaaawww. Eeeees soooo cuuuuuut.' And now their arms brought up small black and silver boxes to cover their faces, from which could be heard an assortment of clicks, whirrs and jingles.

Imvula was most concerned; he must appear more imposing if he was to get any information from these useless creatures. Fortunately he spied a mound of earth piled around the remains of what his mother had informed him the humans called 'fence posts'. If he was to stand upon something they had created, then they must recognise his dominance and so listen to his important question. Never taking his eyes off the vehicle and its jabbering occupants for a moment, Imvula's legs carried him to the mound and, with a sideways shuffle and a quick reverse, got him to the top. Although his ears were quite tired by now, he kept them outstretched and tried to imitate his father.

'People of the vehicle, I, Imvula, soon to be a very big bull, have a question to ask you.' The squawking had died down and they just sat there, mouths open and eyes shining – Imvula thought he might try the look sometime, it was pretty frightening. He took advantage of the pause and continued: 'I have reason to believe that today is going to be a very special day, but nobody will tell me why.' Then, struck by a bright idea, he added, 'If you tell me why today is going to be a very special day, I will remember you all and be very nice to you when I am a big bull. My daddy is a big bull and I know he scares all of you!' How could anyone not tell him now? He was a genius!

Sadly, although Imvula was very clever, it did not seem that the humans were as they were still sitting there with the open mouths and shining eyes. One in the back even had water falling from her eyes – what a waste! (Elephants can tell which humans are boys and which are girls as they smell different.) There was nothing for it; if the humans would not help Imvula, then he would have to charge them. After all, he was a very brave elephant and brave elephants cannot be ignored. He made himself appear very big, stretched his ears even further and launched himself – dislodging stones, dirt and a host of objecting insects – from the top of the mound towards the vehicle.

Something was wrong.

His legs struggled to keep up with his speeding body and the vehicle kept getting larger.

It was stationary.

It was not retreating.

Brakes!

His front legs set rigid and planted themselves among the tufts of grass. The front of his body stopped, but it swayed forward alarmingly as his rear end attempted to do the same and the following wind caught in his outstretched ears, making it only just possible to avoid toppling to the ground. This was almost a total disaster; luckily his trunk gave him courage, leaping out to face the enemy, allowing Imvula time to plan his escape. A brave elephant must, after all, survive to fight another day.

There was no support to be found from his mum or any of his aunts and Imvula could not squeal because Pixle squealed and he was far braver than him. So Imvula reversed for five paces, turned to his right and walked, rather quickly, some might say ran, towards his mother.

'They don't know anything and I am hungry,' he mumbled to Charlie and Pixle as he passed them. His two cousins had emerged from the bush in time to witness the whole sorry affair.

'Better luck next time,' said Pixle, who really meant it, as he was a nice elephant, if slightly timid. Charlie pretended to have ignored the whole thing. These days she very rarely paid any attention to the humans, for she was over two years of age and far too busy to be bothered by them. Despite this, she continued to go close to the vehicle and was secretly very pleased when all of the faces turned in her direction.

With a cough, a strange rattle and a puff of smoke the vehicle burst into life and moved off down the road, disappearing behind the yellow bark of a fever tree. Imvula watched them go before pulling a tuft of grass out of the ground, throwing it onto his head and continuing up the hill towards his mother for milk and a kind word.

'That's nice, dear,' said Curve as she saw the sorrowful, grass-covered figure of her son approach.

'Mum, I am bored of this game now; even the humans won't tell me why today is going to be a very special day.'

'Of course they could not tell you,' Curve replied. 'They do not know either. One thing you must always remember about humans is that though they can be very clever, they have forgotten they are animals and now cannot read the signs of the world around them. Even that young man at the front of the vehicle, the one who is always there, cannot see what is going to happen. I imagine when it is done he will look back and smile that he missed what was so obvious. Try not to hurry things, Imvula, you will discover it all in good time.'

With that, Curve walked towards Constant, rumbling in greeting. The two cows stood face to face, linked trunks and, for a moment, stood completely still. Then, as if finding the answer to an unspoken question, the two began to move slowly towards the ridge of the hill. Charisma, Pixle, Charm and Charlie followed close behind and so Imvula was left without much choice but to take his place within the group and leave behind the disappointment and unanswered questions of the river line.

The night was now just a memory. The sun flew proud in the sky, golden against a backdrop of startling, perfect blue. Black-shouldered kites hovered high above the ground searching for the movement that promised a satisfying meal. All the animals of the plains watched the progress of our little elephant family.

It was another beautiful day in Zululand, but Imvula struggled to carry the weight of the unanswered question: why was it to be a very special day?

The Herd

When you are only a small elephant, you may have big dreams and be driven by the need to answer big questions, but you also have large problems. Your problems are big rocks, cracks in the ground, unexplained mounds of earth blocking otherwise good paths, and all the other obstacles to be found on a long walk. You do not want to go on long walks, you want to feed, play, explore (on your own) and feed again. This explains why Imvula was not in a good mood or paying much attention to what was going on around him as the little group made their way towards a meeting with the sky. Imvula was doing his best not to fall over and face the humiliation of causing the group to stop while a relative's firm trunk extended to help him back in line.

Imvula was, therefore, completely surprised by what lay before him when eventually his little legs had managed to carry the rest of him, including his faithful trunk, to the top of the hill. From this position he could see the whole world. The hill fell away from him to be replaced by another rise, both covered by thousands of trees and promising more food than an elephant could wish for. Beyond the trees gleamed the lake, the place he wanted to be today more than all the sweet grass in the world. On the far side of the lake, propping up the sky, and forming the edge of the world,

were the mountains. But what caused Imvula's mouth to hang open and his trunk to wiggle excitedly were the many elephants he could see feeding below him. They had joined the herd!

All the adults in Imvula's group knew that they were joining the herd, but Imvula had been so concerned with life at his level and the Big Question that he had not paid attention to their rumblings. Elephants have an amazing ability to talk to each over very long distances, as well as when they are close to each other. But they have to concentrate and use more than just their ears if they are to understand the messages, which explains why Imvula had failed to understand the reason for the walk. He was not alone; his cousins were equally clueless. Pixle had been too busy watching the butterflies and even Charlie had been distracted by trying to clean her new tusks with her tongue.

Imvula had been with the herd before, but he never felt quite as big and brave as usual when so many other elephants surrounded him. There were other young bulls there, most of them older than him and not like Pixle at all. In fact, he found himself liking Pixle more when they all spent time with the herd.

Then there was Buga. Like Curve, Buga was a matriarch, but she was in charge of all the female and young male elephants in the reserve. Rumour had it that Buga was the oldest and fiercest elephant in all Africa! She protected the herd from any danger and often chased away the green vehicle with the funny humans. Despite this, as Imvula wandered through the forest of legs, trunks and tusks, he had often heard the older elephants complaining about Buga, saying she was too fierce and that the humans were not that bad. Imvula was sure that fierce was very similar to brave, so he was inclined to like Buga; but he was not sure if she liked him so he did his best to stay out of her way.

On a normal day it was fair to say that Imvula would have had mixed feelings about joining the herd, but this was not an ordinary day and he saw in the meeting a chance to conduct further investigations. By the time this had all gone through his head, his little family were halfway down the hill and approaching the edge of the herd.

As usual, some young males were keeping Shayisa, Buga's twelve-year-old son, company. They, like Imvula, were desperate to become big brave bulls, but were a little nearer to achieving such a stage than Imvula. However, Imvula saw them only as future rivals and so ignored them. All except Shayisa, whom he admired greatly. Shayisa was known to go off on his own sometimes and would only return to the herd when he wanted to; he had even escaped from the reserve and made it back without the humans catching him. Shayisa became aware of Imvula's attentive gaze and greeted him warmly. 'Well, hello there little brother. How goes it with you today?'

'Not well, sir,' replied Imvula, slightly breathlessly. 'Today is a very special day and nobody will tell me why. Will you tell me why? You see, I thought I was the only special one.'

'You are indeed a special one,' Shayisa smiled, stroking his smooth tusk with his trunk, 'but there is room in this world for more than one special thing; just as there is room in this world for both you and I, for are we not both special bulls?' Without waiting for a reply, he continued: 'I think maybe this is a special day the ladies know a little more about than you or I. You must watch them carefully. Run along now, your mother is just about to greet mine.'

When elephants greet each other after a time apart they

are very concerned to show their affection for one another and to inquire as to each other's well being. This they do by rumbling together and constantly touching and smelling each other. Smell tells an elephant so much. Just think how much we can smell with such small noses, now imagine what is on offer to an elephant. This ceremonial greeting gave Imvula the chance to catch up with his mother and so be presented, only slightly reluctantly, to the famous Buga. He stood in the shadow of her bulk and, though he wanted to be very brave, his eyes felt pinned to the ground and he could only manage to stare at her knees.

'Well, boy,' said a deep, but not unkind voice, 'do you not a have a greeting for me?'

'Y-y-yes,' stammered Imvula, desperately trying to remember what not to say. 'Hello-very-scary-chaser-of-vehicles.'

Silence. Imvula felt his mother stiffen, heard the nearby young bulls stifle a giggle and saw Charm smile.

Eventually, though he wished the day to pass and a swift night to come and aid his escape, Imvula raised his head to nervously look at the matriarch.

Her ears were just flapping in the slight breeze, her trunk hung in front of her and, though her face was stern, her eyes carried the same amused expression he remembered in his mother's when she watched him charge small birds or fall in yet another hole.

'I see all I have heard about you is true: only just bigger than a large warthog, but a cheekier than a troop of monkeys. This is all very well for now, but make sure that you learn to use your brains as well as your muscles as passing time allows you to grow. Go on now, I must see your aunts.'

Imvula stood his ground.

'Is there something else?' Buga enquired, an edge to her voice letting Imvula know that she was running out of patience.

'Yes,' he said, setting his jaw with determination, but trying not to meet the hardening look in her huge eyes. 'Why is it a very special day today? Nobody will tell me and I want to know.' It seemed as if every elephant in the area was holding its breath and waiting to see what would be the fate of this young bull who obviously had never been taught manners, or caution.

'Young bulls are not supposed to know everything. If they did, the world would fall apart.'

This was a very unsatisfactory answer indeed, but, before Imvula could reply, his mother ushered him back and away from the tight circle of adults. Glancing back, Imvula could see that Buga was now standing close to Constant, rumbling in the way that only adults can understand, tenderly running her trunk along the underside of Constant's belly. For an elephant that is supposed to be very frightening, she looks friendly enough to me, Imvula thought and his fear decreased at about the same rate as the distance between himself and the matriarch increased.

Having escaped punishment, Imvula was now of no interest to the other elephants and, one by one, heads returned to bushes or trees and began again the search for food. Some of the very young elephants, of a similar age to Imvula, had tired of play and so lay down to sleep. The young bulls who had shadowed Shayisa (and sniggered at Imvula) now fought each other. Clashing tusks, they each tried to force their trunk to press down on the head of the other, or to drive the other back. This looked like fun to Imvula, but they were a bit big for him and, besides, he still needed to find out why this was a very special day.

In search of a good idea, he wandered around trying to spot a clue, or at least someone to help him. Asking the wildebeest would not be a good idea. It was common knowledge that they were stupid and would run in circles for fear of their own shadow. Zebras are rude, impala too shy, and giraffe – who know everything on account of the view they get from the top of their exceedingly long necks – well, there was never one around when you needed one.

Rooting around in a clump of long grass, looking for brightly coloured insects to annoy with blasts of hot air from his trunk, Imvula was suddenly aware of birds falling from the air and landing around him.

Raising his head he stared with alarm at the large white bird with a short yellow beak and beady little eyes that stood before him, head cocked to one side.

'Whatcha got for me?' the egret squawked.

'What?' Imvula knew these birds and knew they were not to be trusted.

'Whatcha got for me? Me and my mates have been watching you and we reckon you have found some of what we want.'

'I have done nothing of the sort,' replied Imvula. Elephants do not talk to egrets, which eat the insects the elephants disturb as they move through the grass, however much they pester them. But Imvula was still only small and he had wandered a little too far from the rest of the herd.

''Ere, lads, we've got a right one 'ere. Thinks he can lie to us, so he does. Come on, come and 'ave a look.'

One by one, more egrets fell from the sky and landed in the long grass. Jabbing their necks in the manner of a dancing Egyptian, they began to advance towards Imvula. There was nothing left to do but fight. So, for the third time that day, and led by his trunk, he charged. But as soon as he got anywhere near his tormentors they would quickly take flight only to land again just behind him. Though his legs were willing and propelled his little body in pursuit, he was just running around in circles and becoming increasingly tired.

Still they came and suddenly it all became a bit much for Imvula – the unanswered question, the long walk, the fearful Buga and now egrets who, confident in their numbers, seemed intent on making him drop down from exhaustion. He was tired and hungry and there was only one other option: he squealed.

We know that Imvula is a very brave little elephant and in her own way so did Curve. She had become used to him wandering off to have various adventures and she knew it was the only way he would learn all that he must know in order to equip him for a future beyond the family. However, he almost never squealed. So, when the sound split the air, her ears fanned and she instantly wheeled to face its direction. In the blink of an eye she went from standing to running and, covering the distance between her and Imvula in a few strides, sent the egrets scattering skywards. They grouped, wheeled, and flew off to land some distance away, where Imvula was sure he could hear their unkind laughter.

'I couldn't get them mum,' he managed to mumble as he once again nestled under her forelegs, searching for the reassuring milk. Curve said nothing; she did not have to – even brave little bulls become afraid sometimes.

Ingani

Hours have now passed since we caught up with Imvula in the thorny darkness of the river line. The sun has climbed in the sky and reached its zenith, the point where it can rise no higher and so must slowly start to fall. Now you must imagine the heat, greater than an English summer can ever provide. It is a time of stillness and quiet.

The only movement is provided by a lazy wind, which, hot itself, merely breaks upon your body and goes no further, bringing little relief. These hours of the day should be slept through (something that the animals and the field rangers both agree upon) for, if you are patient, the sun will continue on its journey to the western sky and the day will cool. Only then will the animals begin to allow themselves to move a little more, emerge from the shade of the bushes and begin to do all those things essential to life that the extreme heat had previously made impossible.

During these quiet, hot hours many of the elephants sleep, though some must stay awake to watch for any approaching danger. They all stand very still, so still that after a while it is possible to believe that all of the real elephants have somehow crept away and left only statues in their place. The only sound to be heard, apart from the background chorus of thousands of crickets – ever present and so almost forgotten – is a slow, regular *thwack*. This sound, as constant as the swinging pendulum of an ancient clock, is produced when a large, leathery and vein-lined ear slowly slaps against the mass of a great shoulder, seeking to cool the hot elephant blood contained within.

The herd had begun to move away, their numbers spreading out towards the top of a hill. In time, they would head in the direction of the wooded valley whose steep sides prevented any approach by the humans, guaranteeing peace and shade from the powerful sun. Curve, however, showed no desire to want to follow this movement and so her family remained on the slopes of the hill, near a grove of knobthorn trees, standing close together and very still.

Imvula wanted to sleep. Having forgotten his troubles with the egrets and possessing a belly full of milk it was very difficult not to follow the example of Pixle, who lay at the feet of his mother, lost in the dreams of a deep sleep. Even Charlie was swaying slightly, which Imvula knew to be the last stage before she too forgot her desire to be an adult, let her rear end collapse, and settled comfortably on the warm earth. Imvula, however, could not afford to sleep as time was running out and he was very aware that he still had no idea why this day was special above any other.

In an effort to fight the heaviness that tugged at his eyelids and seemed to pull his head towards the ground, Imvula moved away from the circle of elephants and edged a little further into the grove of knobthorn trees. Simply stepping away from the group was enough to banish the heaviness of sleep from his eyes, for he had to be alert as he adjusted to the shade and peered past the staunch tree trunks to see what lurked within.

The knobthorns were trees found all across the reserve. Imvula fondly remembered a recent time when they had bloomed with beautiful yellow flowers, blessed with a smell so sweet he and his trunk had spent much of their time just letting the wind overpower them with the gifts of the trees. The knobthorns grew quite tall, though nothing to match the yellow fever trees or the vibrant green of the brackthorn, and carried thorns everywhere. The knobs that covered the trunk were each topped with a vicious spike and thorns stood tall throughout all the branches. The thorns prevented animals from eating the trees and though they could prevent the antelope, they were no match for an elephant. The elephants love knobthorns; they eat the leaves, enjoy the twigs and even strip long lengths of bark to feast on the hidden sweetness which nestles between the tree's outer coat and its heartwood.

Imvula should therefore not have been surprised to find an elephant already there, but what he saw made butterflies flutter from the milk in his belly and his normal confidence turn to uncertainty. There, in the shade of the trees, was a greater darkness, one that blocked the light from the surrounding sky and breathed with a slow rise and fall of his massive body. Legs, thicker than the surrounding tree trunks, rose to support a body of unbelievable proportions. Though the skin was wrinkly and loose – like that of all elephants – it looked like a sheet thrown over an expanse of twisted muscle, incapable of concealing the tremendous strength contained within.

The curve of the elephant's back rose to a peak over his powerful shoulders and then fell towards the gentle slope of his head. Imvula was unable to stop staring. The broad forehead ended with two large hollows, supported by a ridge that in turn protected the now closed eyes and fell like the sides of an oversized hourglass to the sheath of the tusks. The trunk was thick, layered, and hung so low that a

good portion of it rested on the earth. Yet all of this wonder was insignificant when placed against the magnificent tusks. These broad sweeps of sharpened ivory began somewhere under the sleeping trunk and stretched far out to a point clear of the gigantic animal. The left tusk sought to reach the ground before the right one and so swept low. The right tusk had kept its height, but gained a groove that scored across a few centimetres from the tip, as if in opposition to any further growth.

Imvula let these wonderful details linger on his eye and sink into his mind, for he was looking at Ingani and at the promise of his future.

Imvula had found his father.

Bull elephants do not spend all of their days with their families. They must patrol the whole of the reserve searching for food and keeping an eye on what the other bulls are doing. This meant that Imvula did not see a lot of his father and so was filled with awe whenever his silhouette marked the horizon, or an ear-splitting *crack!* filled the air as a once proud tree toppled to the ground, telling the small family that Ingani and his enormous strength were near. Imvula did not know how his father spent his days, but he did know that he must eventually follow the same path and it thrilled him to know that one day he would grow to such a size.

At that moment the wind gathered and, in an attempt at activity, blew fitfully from Imvula towards his father. The slack trunk twitched and a large eye slowly opened. But the wind had quickly died and so it took the opening of the other eye, plus a moment of concentration, before Ingani could make out the figure of the small elephant. The figure was hesitating in the gap between a young knobthorn and the smooth thin branches of a raisin bush, now carrying only a few dried husks of the berries that Ingani fondly remembered eating eagerly just a few months back. Though the wind no longer told its tale, the young elephant's small size and the battle between fear and courage betrayed by his face told the bull that this could only be his small son. So, with a shift of his mass sending a gentle ripple throughout his body, and banishing sleep for the time being, Ingani waited to see what news this little messenger brought.

Ingani was not an old bull – a fact reflected by his name. Ingani, in the language of the Zulu, means child. Though he had long outgrown his name, it tells us that Ingani was closer to youth than old age. Though he carried long tusks and heavily wrinkled skin, everything about him shouted his status as a young, strong bull. His movements were easy and flowed like running water, never interrupted by the cautious hesitation of the old, who do not trust their strength or ability to walk on unsure surfaces without stumbling. Humans did not concern him and he preferred to use the roads they had cut through the bush, confident that their vehicles would move out of his way should he meet one.

I ngani remembered well what it was like to be a young elephant and he was particularly fond of Imvula, for what bull forgets his firstborn son? 'I see you Imvula, but only just,' he rumbled. 'Come closer, little man, and tell me how you are.'

Imvula was delighted. Not only did his father want to speak with him, but also there was no one else around to steal his attention. What started out as a casual amble soon developed into an excited scramble as he followed the twists of the small path and came to a rest somewhere below Ingani's knees. The gigantic trunk had gained some life and now gently traced the outline of Imvula's back with its tip, avoiding Imvula's trunk – which stood excitedly before him trying to reach his father – and blew tenderly into the small elephant's mouth.

Overcome by this unexpected attention, Imvula's mind raced as he tried to decide what to tell his father; so much had happened that day. There was the aardvark, his fight with Pixle, annoying Charlie, the excitement of meeting the herd and that little incident with the egrets. But it seemed that the decision was made for him, for before he knew it he heard himself ask breathlessly, 'Mum says that today is a special day, but she won't tell me why. She says that I must find out for myself if I am to grow to be a bull who is clever as well as strong. But I do not have any idea and I have tried so hard, even keeping my eyes open all day when everybody else is sleeping. I do so want to know because otherwise I cannot become a big brave bull like you and I want to be like you.'

This last sentence came out in a rush, for bulls are not supposed to admit to failure, but by now Imvula's growing frustration was a little more than he could handle.

While listening to his son's plea, Ingani's trunk curled around the base of a tuft of dry grass, pulled and removed the whole thing, roots and all, from the earth. Lifting the clump in the air, trailing stones and dust, he absent-mindedly shook the roots free of soil and dropped them onto his back, where they clung until slipping silently onto Imvula below. Ingani had heard the catalogue of rumbles that had passed back and forth between the female elephants since the beginning of the day. He recognised the elephants' pattern of movement, which had recently changed, and understood enough of the rumbles to know what was soon to happen. However, he also understood why Curve had not told Imvula what was to happen and why his son was

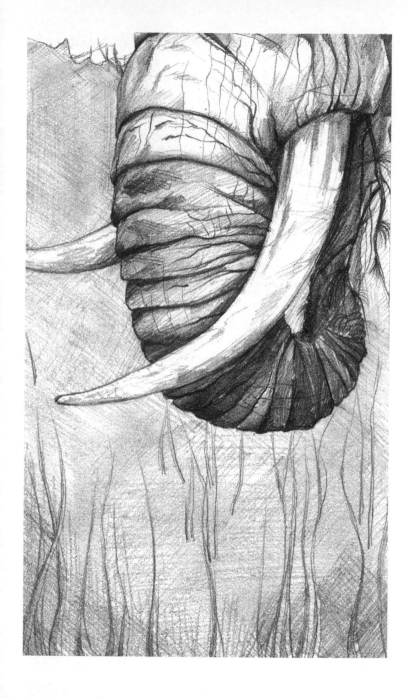

so desperate to know. He would have to be careful in his reply.

'Well, my little bull,' Ingani began slowly, conscious that what he was to say might disappoint the little figure at his feet, but sure that he was right, 'it is not my place to go against what your mother says. She is the one that you must look to for answers to questions that arise every day and so if she tells you something, then she has her reasons and I do not doubt them.'

'But that is what they have all said, even Auntie Constant!' blurted out Imvula, who at that moment began to try to stem the tears that threatened to overwhelm his eyelids and trail down his cheeks. I hate all this dust he thought, blinking away the tears. It must be the dust; brave elephants don't cry.

'There you go, rushing off again, attacking what you do not understand.' Ingani was unconcerned by his son's outburst and pressed on with what he had to say, slightly unsure – for this was the first time that he had been called upon to be a wise elephant. He cast his mind back to Induna, the biggest bull of all. Induna was old, wise and, most importantly, patient; his huge head held all the world's knowledge. In recent years, since his arrival from the land beyond the western mountains, he had been trying to share this wisdom with Ingani. Now it was the time to pass it on to his son.

'I will not tell you what is to happen, but I will tell you that it does not matter if what happens catches you by surprise and unprepared. You will still grow to be a big bull, though whether you are brave and wise is up to you.

'At the moment, your days are full of playing and eating. When you are tired you go close to your mother and fall asleep, content that she will keep you safe and warm. There is nothing wrong with this, because that is the way of things. But by not preparing you for this special day, your mother is telling you that there is more to our lives than you know. You must learn to walk with open eyes and take care to know the health and well-being of the elephants who move with you. You must be ready for extraordinary events and know that they will not always be expected or understood. Whatever happens, you must be prepared to respond, for others will always look to you.'

Ingani paused to see if Imvula understood what he said and continued: 'You are a bull and if the land remains kind and danger passes you by then you will grow to be as big as me, maybe even bigger.' This caught Imvula's attention and he stared at the gleaming ivory of his father's tusks, unable to believe that he would ever be the proud owner of anything like them. 'You will walk a lonely path and so must possess the wisdom and knowledge to cope with whatever you meet on that road. Though it will be many years before that time, it is important that your eyes are open now.

'I have walked beyond the wire fence that blocks our way and so one day, when all the fences fall – as fall they must, for nothing humans make lasts for ever – then you will walk that way too. On the other side of the fence there are many more humans, their vehicles move faster and the trees have fallen away. Only with knowledge and open eyes will you survive this land to be a father yourself someday.'

Imvula's breathing had become deep and regular and his head dropped slightly. Ingani smiled when he saw that his son slept. There was no need to wake the little one. The lesson would be repeated many more times until, one day, all would change and the student would become the teacher.

A New Beginning

Sleep did not hold Imvula for long; he did not dream and was soon awake, happy to see that his father remained. Side by side they left the cover of the trees and emerged into the light of the afternoon.

A dust cloud moving along the road in the distance told the elephants of the nearness of the humans and their vehicle, but it passed by and was ignored by the family who remained still, standing in a tight group. Ingani, seeing that he was not needed, said goodbye to Imvula and moved away along the path to the road and the crest of the hill. He would now go to find the herd and feast on the stubby aloes – curious angular plants, growing to half his size, with glorious explosions of colour for flowers, and which grew among the rocks of the wooded valleys.

Imvula watched his father's progress. The four massive feet were placed carefully so close to one another on the path that the body appeared barely balanced by this arrangement and swayed from side to side with every step taken. Dust rose in billows as the earth absorbed the passing weight of this Lord of the Bush, softening his outline, easing the change from elephant to memory. Increasing distance made him appear gradually smaller until finally he was gone. Imvula always felt a little sad when his father left. Sometimes he found it difficult to remember if Ingani had

really been with him at all, or whether his nearness was just a nice dream. Fortunately, on this day, large circular tracks, criss-crossed with miniature ridges made of dust drawn from the cracks in the soles of Ingani's feet, reassured Imvula that his father had indeed been with him, sharing the shade of the trees in the knobthorn grove.

If the meeting had happened, then his father's advice was also a reality that must be followed. So he turned to observe his family with the new eyes of the brave adventurer and protector, cast in the image of his father, that he must grow to be.

But nothing seemed to have changed. Even leaning slightly forward and squinting with the effort of concentration made no difference. Pixle and Charlie remained lying on their side and his mother and aunts continued to stand in a group. They remained motionless, the stillness of the picture broken only by the darting black specks of attentive flies and the regular but slow flap of individual ears.

'Look again!' commanded a grey lourie, perched high in one of the knobthorns that bordered the grove. This grey bird, proud of its crested plume, was known throughout the bush for telling everyone what to do and once it began sharing its advice it was very difficult to stop. 'Look again!' the lourie repeated. Imvula swung his trunk in frustration but, concentrating madly, began to see that something was indeed different.

There was a sense of expectation in the air. It hung heavily, reached down and woke Pixle and Charlie from their dreams. They raised their heads, struck rigid forelegs out into the dirt in front of them and struggled to their feet. Looking around groggily, they did what all young elephants do when they are unsure of what is happening and ambled to their mothers. Charlie, too old to feed, rubbed against

Charm to feel the comfort of her mother's touch. Pixle, trying his luck, attempted to feed but was pushed impatiently away by Charisma. He squealed, but only managed to scare a flock of small aquilas into the air from their perch in the twisted remains of an old scented thorn tree. Surprised by their rejection, the two small elephants stood close to one another, in between Imvula and the adults, and also tried to discover what had changed.

Curve and Constant stood so close that they appeared to have become one elephant. Imvula noticed that his aunt seemed to be distracted and agitated. Her head was raised and her back slightly arched, but her ears remained flat against her head. The other elephants did not warn of danger, or gather the young to them – as was the custom when the group felt threatened. Curve stood eye to eye with her sister, her trunk busy. Linking first with Constant's trunk, it then slipped free to investigate her mouth and touch her cheek, belly and chest with slight, gentle movements of the tip.

Charisma and Charm stood either side of the central pair, facing towards Constant. The family had no attention for anything other than this sense of anticipation, which seemed to come from the very centre of the group though it continued to hide its identity from the fascinated Imvula. The four elephants began to sway, gradually losing their individual identity, appearing like a ship rolling heavily over the waves of a mighty ocean. The heat of the day remained, though the fierceness of the midday sun was now some hours past. Ears were extended and then brought back in order to create currents of air to cool the constantly moving animals.

Constant leant on Curve, trusting that her sister's strength would be enough to support much of her weight.

Imvula could see from the rise and slope of her back that she was also resting the leg which carried the unhealed wound. Charisma and Charm rocked back and forth, seemingly trying to restrain their darting trunks, and as close to Constant as it was possible to be without touching.

Imvula became aware of a rumble coming from the family. It rolled outwards, across the ground until, meeting him, it climbed up and over, pressing at his throat and filling his ears. This was a rumble that Imvula had never heard before. In fact he did not hear it, but felt it, such was its force. Leaves fluttered, though there was no wind and the ants, scorpions and many legged creatures left their daily chores and ducked back into their holes. Birds did not fly from the trees in fright, but remained where they were, as if stuck by some invisible glue. All the eyes of the animals on that hillside turned to stare at the family. Imvula was alone in not knowing the meaning of that rumble; all the world seemed to pause and hold its breath for what was to follow.

The rumbles were echoed time and time again until Imvula felt tempted to check the sky for signs of a distant thunderstorm. He had become rooted to the ground and knew that he must not move until the end of whatever was happening. This must be the special event which had shaped this day. This would be the event that helped him become the bull he so wished to be. This was something he could not afford to miss one little detail of. He stood a few paces from his mother and trembling aunt, but he swayed with them, linked by unseen ties. And though he held his eyes wide, it became impossible for him to make out the individual elephants, to decide where one ended and the other began.

The rumbles increased, moving back and forth between the closely swaying elephants, bouncing off bodies and rippling outwards, escaping into the space of the bush to tell of the arrival of the spirit of the elephant. Suddenly these layers of sound were split in two as a deafening trumpet left Constant's trunk and seemed to be hurled high into the afternoon sky. She stopped moving and stood completely still, front legs slightly apart and shoulders braced.

Then silence.

The trees absorbed the final ripples of the once thunderous rumbles. The sound of the trumpet had flown far into the sky and now arched way beyond the horizon.

Imvula waited.

The world waited.

Curve shifted backwards and allowed a crack of light to appear between Constant and herself. She gazed steadily as Constant, slowly swinging her head twice from side to side, then turned slightly, looking down to the ground beneath her. The grass below, which had been standing proud, shooting up from the collection of cracked, brown rocks, was now flattened and disturbed. It was to this area of disturbance that Constant's head was drawn, where her trunk investigated with the most tender of touches and where even her tusks, normally tools and weapons, became gentle supports.

Imvula watched all of this with a growing sense of wonder. Although he was concerned that any movement would cause the rumbling and swaying to begin again immediately, his curiosity proved stronger than his fear. Four paces closer he could see now the detail of the scene surrounding his mother and favourite aunt. There, at Constant's feet, Imvula could see the slight rise of a small grey mound.

The mound suddenly moved; a small twitch met the gentle pressure of Constant's tusks. The twitch was not the springing-back movement expected of a branch after it has been pushed to one side. Nor was it the crack of a rotten log as it gave way under some unbearable weight. Nor did it tell of the settling of soil piled too high outside somebody's hole. All of these things Imvula had seen for himself and understood, but this movement was different. This movement was a twitch and Imvula knew that only living things twitch and that meant only one thing – the Spirit of the Elephant had brought with it new life.

The barrier of grass disappeared as it was trampled closer to the earth and Imvula was slowly able to see the details of this life. Life was covered in wrinkles, still wet from the passage of his birth. The four legs were at that moment stretching and marvelling in the freedom with which they could move. The head took comfort from the warmth of a rock, smoothed by its journey through a million years, and only shifted to enjoy the shadow cast by Constant. Imvula, bolder now and very close, could see one large eye shining from beneath the baby's long lashes. The eye blinked constantly and Imvula remembered the shock of entering a world of light from the place of warm dark; a shock that it was now his small cousin's task to face.

Imvula moved even closer to Constant, but the firm trunk of his mother prevented him from getting any nearer. 'Not now dear,' his mother murmured, 'you cannot demand all of your aunt's attention now, she must look after her own son.'

The new addition to the family had gained his feet and unsteadily surveyed his new world from the top of his four legs, which for the first time were expected to hold his weight and even move him from one place to another. He gazed at the elephants surrounding him and made his first small attempts at movement. These brought him into contact with Curve, who gently pushed him back towards Constant before Imvula could touch his young cousin. Like all young elephants, nothing could be more important than fulfilling the urge to feed when his stomach decided it was time. Knowing that the answer lay with his mother, the newborn elephant lay his limp trunk across his raised head and tottered towards Constant. But he was unsure as to the exact position of the milk and so first he bumped into her two forelegs, one, then the other, before being ushered to her chest by the firm guidance of both Constant and Curve's trunks.

Constant seemed a little unsure of what was happening. Her ears were spread as if in alarm and she continually made small movements, first forwards, then backwards; all the while swinging her head to keep an eye on the small life that stumbled below her. Curve remained close, reassuring her sister with the occasional touch but gently encouraging her to move.

Whatever extraordinary events happen during the course of an elephant's day, they must continue to eat if their large bodies are going to gain the energy they need. During the hours leading to the birth, the family had eaten little. Now the heat of the day was fading and the time was right to move, to find food and shelter where the new life could spend his first night. These thoughts were in Curve's mind as she followed the route taken earlier by both the herd and Ingani and led the little group along the much travelled path.

So the small family, travelling in a tight cluster and alert for the slightest danger, climbed the hill, crossed the dusty slash of the human road and slipped into the safety of the sickle thicket. There the sickle bushes grew tall and thick, offering food and safety. Charm and Charisma began to feed with enthusiasm. Curve picked occasionally at the

offered branches, more concerned with Constant who stood quietly, enjoying the touch of the elephant who was her long-awaited son. She raised her head, smiling contentedly and announced to any who listened: 'My son is dry already from the waters that eased his birth. He has been born at a time when rain is just a memory and even the landing of a single beetle brings forth a small cloud of dust. But the dry is not bad, for it provides a balance to the wet; both are required for life to prosper. My nephew is Imvula, therefore my son must be called Omile, the dry one.'

Imvula watched all of this from his position on the edge of the group. He was used to being the centre of attention, confident that of all the family, he was the special one. Now another small elephant stood at the centre of the group. But Imvula was not angry or sad, though maybe he did feel a little jealous. Instead he understood that this was a very special day for him as well as for the little family. Now Omile must be the one to cherish memories of the darkness and the warmth of his beginning; Imvula must heed the lessons of his father and look to the future. He must learn what is sweet to eat and strive to grow as big and strong as Ingani. He must listen to the wisdom of his mother and seek the company of his father. He must try to learn the lessons contained within the book of nature and bear patiently the challenges of life in his world.

So now, at the close of this very special day, we must leave Imvula in a similar manner to how we found him: battling his way through the closely packed spines of a sickle thicket, his trunk sniffling through the grass and fallen leaves, his brain pondering the future.

In your mind, leave the thicket and fly with me into the air. The reserve is preparing for the coming night. The sun has set in blinding gold, which makes the riches of men pale

in comparison. Light slowly drains away, following the dropping sun, and the sky darkens. One by one, stars sparkle, waiting for the last of the purple mountains to disappear before they reveal their full glory. The frogs join the crickets in the evening chorus and across the reserve the occasional light can be seen as the humans once again try to mimic the stars.

The day has ended, but another will follow and another, until maybe one day you will join the little family of elephants in the Pongola Game Reserve.

And that, to be sure, will be a very special day.

The End

Update

Although Imvula was absolutely serious about the promises that he made to himself on that very special day, he remains a young elephant with many years in front of him before he grows to such a size that he must walk the paths alone.

I have it on very good authority that having grown used to his young cousin, Imvula continues to face life as a very brave and very inquisitive elephant. There is not an animal alive in the bush that he confesses to be afraid of. The day is not complete unless he has had at least one fight with the reluctant Pixle. Charlie still takes herself very seriously indeed. As for the humans and their big green vehicle, well, few people return home without having faced the bravely spread ears and raised trunk of our hero. Yet he still takes great comfort from the touch of his mother and longs for the visits of his father.

A very brave elephant indeed.

Acknowledgements

Anyone who has ever had the privilege to spend time in the company of elephants will know the diversity and magnitude of the feelings they are capable of invoking. This little story is an attempt to share the elephant's mysterious majesty, which captured me for the priceless months that it was my pleasure to spend in the Pongola Game Reserve, KwaZulu-Natal, and that holds me still.

So it is with immense gratitude that I acknowledge the help, guidance, support and patience of everyone at the Reserve and, specifically at the White Elephant Safari Lodge and Bush Camp, without which I would have been completely – and quickly – lost.

Finally, I would like to endorse the work of the Space for Elephants Foundation. Only by entwining conservation with development will either prosper; as in the old Zulu tale, where it is said that when two sticks are bound together they are harder to break.

3814035R00046

Printed in Great Britain
by Amazon.co.uk, Ltd.,
Marston Gate.